FELIX and the MONSTERS

JOSH and MONICA HOLTSCLAW

 NANCY PAULSEN BOOKS

NANCY PAULSEN BOOKS

An imprint of Penguin Random House LLC, New York

Copyright © 2020 by Josh Holtsclaw and Monica Holtsclaw

Library of Congress Cataloging-in-Publication Data
Names: Holtsclaw, Josh, author, illustrator. | Holtsclaw, Monica, author, illustrator.
Title: Felix and the monsters / Josh and Monica Holtsclaw.
Description: New York: Nancy Paulsen Books, [2020] | Summary: "A lonely guard's love for music leads him to discover what's actually on the other side of the wall he's guarding"—Provided by publisher.
Identifiers: LCCN 2019043557 | ISBN 9780593110522 (hardcover) | ISBN 9780593110546 (kindle edition) | ISBN 9780593110539 (epub) | Subjects: CYAC: Security guards—Fiction. | Musicians—Fiction. | Monsters—Fiction. | Classification: LCC PZ7.1.H649 Fel 2020 | DDC [E]—dc23
LC record available at https://lccn.loc.gov/2019043557

Manufactured in China.
ISBN 9780593110522
10 9 8 7 6 5 4 3 2 1

Design by Nicole Rheingans | Text set in Cheltenham ITC Pro
The illustrations were created using a combination of handmade mixed-media textures and digital painting.

*For our friends, family,
and all of the kids in our lives:
Aliyah, Colin, Marin, and Ollie.*

FELIX was a guard at the wall. On the other side lived horrible little monsters. It was his job to keep them out.

Well, that was the job title on his business card.

The other guards actually *guarded* the wall.

Felix mostly liked to play his keytar and daydream about being in a band.

boop.
boop.

There is nothing sadder than
a keytarist without a band.

Felix asked the other guards
if they would jam with him.

"Never gonna happen," the head guard said. "We're here to guard! That's what we have always done, and what we will always do. If you have a problem with that, maybe you need a different job!"

Felix *wanted* a different job. He knew
he wasn't meant to be a guard.

That afternoon, he played a moody
song on his keytar.

He was swept up in one of the most epic solos *ever* when he heard a THRUM THRUM THRUM coming from the top of the wall. He looked up and saw . . . a little monster.

"Hey, um, halt, or . . . wait. Is that a bass guitar?" asked Felix as he climbed up the wall. "Who are you?"

"I'm Dot, from the other side, lured here by the beautiful sounds of that portable piano machine!"

"It's called a keytar," said Felix.

"Are you a musician too?"

"Yup! Wanna jam?"

Felix nodded, and Dot counted
them in by shouting . . .

"HAAALT!
Who goes there?"
yelled another
guard down below.

"Oh no! What do we do?" Felix whispered.

"Come with me to the other side," Dot said.

"But aren't there horrible monsters over there?" Felix asked.

"Hey! I'm not horrible," Dot said. "C'mon!"

So Felix followed Dot into another world.

Felix could not believe his eyes.
All around him, the monsters were
doing all sorts of interesting things—

playing instruments, painting,
and even reciting poetry.

One of them was carving an
elephant out of cheddar cheese.

"How did you *do* that?" asked Felix.

"I simply removed all the bits of cheddar that weren't elephant," replied the little monster.

Felix felt more at home than ever before.

Dot introduced Felix to a few of her friends.

"This is Plink. He's a sax man. And meet Block.

She speaks with her drums."

They exchanged friendly nods.

"Let's jam!" Dot shouted, and counted them in.

But before Dot could count to four, she was interrupted by the sound of yelling guards.

"FELIX! We're coming to save you!"

They climbed the wall, ready to fight.

"What do we do?"
Dot asked.

"The only thing we
can do," Felix answered.

"Play!"

4!
3
2
1

At the sound of their sweet licks, the guards
stopped in their tracks. They had never heard
such beautiful music.

They laid down their spears and danced
the kind of weird dancing you only do when
you think no one is looking.

"Wow! We really misjudged you," said the head guard. "Honestly, the only thing horrible over here is . . . our dancing."

"We weren't going to mention that," Dot said.

"Hear, hear," said the head guard.
"I think it's my turn to find a new job.
What d'ya say we take this wall down?"
Everyone agreed and so they did,
brick by brick.

Then the two sides decided to celebrate together. They used some of the bricks to build a stage for the band to perform on, featuring Felix on the keytar, Dot on the bass guitar, Plink on the saxophone, and Block on the drums.

There's nothing better than
a keytarist with a band of friends.